THEY CAME BACK

STORIES FROM THE RADIUS

The Lost Tales of Science Fiction Writer

RON COLLINS

SKYFOX
PUBLISHING
Science Fiction

Contents

For the stories lost in time

and the ghosts of teachers past

Foreword

"How do you pronounce your name?" I asked the editor in an email.

To my credit, or at least for my benefit, this was in 1994. *Radius* was a very new magazine, and the name Ewan Grantham was unknown to me before it popped up in the online forum I frequented.

All right, it was CompuServe.

Is that what you wanted to hear?

Yes, I am that old.

In 1994 I was a mainstay on the CompuServe writer's forums, a proud wearer of badge #2 in the CompuServe IMPs (which stood for IMPatiently waiting to be published) after I had been the first to respond to Bill Cornett's impassioned plea to start a group for people who hadn't gotten into the CompuServe Writer's Workshop. Long Live King Cornett. He had no idea what he'd just done, but, yea, verily, it was good.

Anyway.

This is not a story about CompuServe, or the IMPs.

It is, however, a story about online publishing, because it turns out that Ewan Grantham had a radical, out-there idea and wanted to try it out. Hence was born *Radius* magazine, about which I'll explain more in a little while.

But first, to the story I opened with.

I was, you see, curious. I wanted to know how to pronounce "Ewan" because I knew, per Dale Carnegie, that it was important to know how to properly pronounce a person's name. Since I was a bit of a sheltered midwestern kid by culture (which is fair to interpret as another way to say *un*cultured), I could concoct a couple of different pronunciations. It seemed like a perfectly fine question.

Still, this is not exactly the most professional thing a new writer can do with an editor.

The answer that came back, however, was one that I'll remember for as long as I have such a thing as the ability to remember anything.

He said: *You pronounce it "the guy who just bought your first story."*

That is a fun way to make your first sale, now, isn't it?

***

That story was a work titled "The Spearhead." It's a far-future space story that weaves its basic narrative together with Hopi mythology—which I am 100% certain came about because Lisa (my wife, sweetie, and life partner for eternity) and I had just driven cross country and spent some time at the Grand Canyon, where I picked up a book or two on Hopi history.

As is only natural, when he bought that story, I sent him another—which he immediately bought, too. This one was "A Corner of the Mind," a Christmas in space story that I liked.

Anyway, *Radius* published "The Spearhead" in October of that year.

"A Corner of the Mind" came out in December. The checks cleared. I was stoked.

Unfortunately, I received an email shortly thereafter from *the guy who just bought your first story.* The magazine wasn't going to make it. *Radius,* he said, was going to publish one more issue, then close shop. And, he asked, did I have anything I thought was good enough to go in his last issue?

Of course, I did. I immediately sent him "Night School," a story that originated in a dream I'd had.

I note that this series of events also makes the oddly pronounced Ewan Grantham the first editor to ever commission a piece from me. I have never met Mr. Grantham, and I've long since lost track of him. My semi-focused Googling to find him has come up dry. But if I ever do run into him, I owe him a beer.

Of course, the counter to this argument is that, like the ephemeral Mr. Grantham, the three stories are now gone. Lost to history, as they say. Vamoosed. Disappeared. They are AWOL, now. They've dropped into the sea of time without leaving a ripple.

This is because, unlike normal publications, *Radius* magazine was truly a piece of radical thinking.

It was, you see, among the first-ever electronic publications.

Taking it a step further, the magazine was delivered in a Windows Help File format.

Which, as hard as it might be to believe, in that moment that was 1994, was more than a little interesting.

Quite intriguing. Kind of fun. This was before anyone had decided online fiction could work at all, so the idea of a help file, delivered in email, that you could open right there on your desktop (because, let's face it, laptops were not the thing then, and phones were still things that almost everyone had tethered to their desks, and that no one could use to read anything on), well, it was almost cool, you know? A techie solution to a techie genre. I enjoyed the heck out of being part of it.

The problem, though, was this delivery method meant there was no archive out there in the nether space of the Information Superhighway. And then it also meant that as Windows tweaked its product, the newer versions of the operating systems eventually stopped being able to read those old files. So those three stories in those three issues sank to the bottom of the Sea of Time and were lost forever.

Until now, anyway.

***

Of course, there's more.

***

I'm adding one more lost story to this book.

It's a tale that makes me giddy with joy.

In these pages, for the first time, you'll find "The Robbery," which is a story I wrote back in high school. I came upon it recently, accompanied by an amazingly kind letter from my teacher's assistant at the time. As I'll discuss in more detail when I get there, the note said the story was good, and encouraged me to set it aside for a little while and come back to it.

Which now, at least a little while later, I've done.

I hope you enjoy both "The Train Robbery," presented in its full form as originally written, as well as "The Hero," which is my effort to update the story all these many years later.

What great fun this was!

***

Finally, a big thank you to you!

Thank you for being a part of this project.

I've been wanting to find a fun way to make this book happen for a long time but couldn't quite decide how I wanted to do it.

Then along came Kickstarter, which ironically, while no longer daring enough to be called a cutting-edge platform anymore, is still early enough in its use as a distribution technology to be considered close to pioneering. Or at least dangerous to folks who grow angsty about dipping their toes into it. But, after running a successful project, it struck me that this approach is perfect for this kind of effort, which I'm titling *They Came Back, Stories from the Radius.* The project is half product, half celebration, and—as far as I'm concerned—all one great full-blooded event. Kickstarter is great for this kind of thing. I absolutely love the idea of bringing these stories back from the depths of obscurity, gussying them up a touch, giving them brand-new packaging, and then shining a light on them in hopes they find new homes.

So, I hope you enjoy these stories.

In getting them together and making them ready for publication, I've fallen in love with them again.

The whole idea just makes me happy.

And, wherever he is, I hope it makes The Guy Who Bought Your First Story Grantham happy, too.

Ron Collins
2023, Las Vegas

The Spearhead

Stark lights dazzled Haggerty's eyes as he stepped through the briefing room's doorway. He blinked and shook his head gently. Normally, the lights didn't bother him. But then, it wasn't normal for him to be shaken out of the rack at 3:00 a.m. for a mission, either.

General Richard sat behind the small briefing table, his face drawn with lines that ran down his cheeks to pool in dark shadows of razor stubble. His eyes were bloodshot, and his monkey suit was creased and stained with coffee and sweat. The General nodded at Haggerty's entry and motioned for him to take a seat.

Haggerty cleared his throat as he lowered himself into the chair next to Dog Cunningham. Once situated, Haggerty—call name, Night Hag— noticed that his escort had closed the door behind him, leaving him alone with Dog and the General.

The General took a shallow breath and pursed his lips into a tight line before he started. "I will be brief and to the point, gentlemen. At 0130, the

Eurasian Space Force officially proclaimed ownership of Space Station Sua."

Haggerty sat stunned.

"There's only a brief window of opportunity left to retaliate. Within two hours, the EAs will be able to override our protection codes. Then, Sua's full arsenal and capability will be at their fingertips." The General stood and, despite his fatigue, strutted to the holoprojector. "Gentlemen, we cannot let that happen."

* * *

The muffled footsteps of six men filled the dimly lit maintenance bay. Two MPs led Haggerty and Dog, and two trailed. It was a quick walk—no discussion, no deviation from their path, no time to think about the twelve hundred Union-loyal people who operated Sua. The bombers awaited.

Haggerty glanced over at Dog. The kid's jaw was set. His eyes glistened in the weak light. He was good but green. Not like Ghostman. But Ghost had been blitzed over the moon a scant few days ago—lucky as hell to still be alive. However, all of Ghostman's luck still wouldn't relieve him of the quarantine required after a stint on the radioactive side of the moon.

That meant that Dog Cunningham would pair with him on the most important mission of his life. Sua was more than just a space station. She was a damned icon—important beyond her value as a key defense point, important beyond being stuffed with more firepower than an entire city on Earth. Named for the lead scientist of the design team who crafted her, she allowed the Union to put masses into space for the first time—something the Eurasians still couldn't do. Sua was the first colonial station, the flagship, and the pride of the Union Space Force.

Some even say that Sua's launch was the first step toward war.

The small group stepped out of the maintenance bay and onto the flight line. Two bombers perched in readiness.

Haggerty looked at his wingman once again. "Take it easy, Dog. Just another ride in the park."

The kid swallowed and craned his neck toward Haggerty. "My father and mother died in Sicily, Night Hag. This is not just another mission."

Sicily. Haggerty's lips became a straight line across his face. Sicily, site of the Holiday Massacre, a brazen act where the Sicilian government rounded up and executed two hundred and twelve vacationing Union citizens, then called it an unfortunate, localized eruption of emotions. That same government had no answer a day later when satellite photos and hand-held videos indicated Italian soldiers were among the killers.

"I'm sorry. Let's go do some business."

Haggerty studied his ship's load-out as he climbed to the cockpit. Limited fuel, lots of anti-air munitions, rockets, a series of laser shields, and a pair of nuclear-powered torpedoes. It would do. He donned his helmet, snapped the visor in place, and ran through the diagnostic checklist. The translucent glow of the ship's registers rode on his visor, telling him everything about the status of his craft.

Everything was go.

He gave Dog a crisp, three-fingered salute that ended with a wave toward the launch bay doors and watched as his wingman returned it. The crew scurried out of the vacuum area.

The launch doors slid open, moving with the graceful aura of uniform speed. In less than a minute he stared out at black, star-speckled space.

The flight commander's voice disturbed the peace of the moment. "All signals *go* for launch."

Haggerty depressed three touchpad sensors and the machine around him shuddered with the power of the engines. He pushed against the torso restraints. He loved that sensation—the uniform pressure of the harness across his shoulders and chest, his legs held in place with Velcro pads. Cold sweat trickled from his armpits, accompanying the rising beat of his heart and the rasp of his breath. The small hairs at the base of his neck stood on end, tickling him, and sending a shiver down his spine.

Seconds later they were ejected. One trip around the base and Haggerty and Dog were formed up and on a direct path to Sua.

* * *

The station loomed ahead, a slowly rotating spindle with the living sphere nestled amidst an outer ring that housed the station's primary power conduits and point defensive systems. Their flight plan was direct and simple. They approached under communications silence but without long-range electromagnetic cover. If they were in time, the straightforward approach would be indefensible. Otherwise, the mission would fail anyway.

Haggerty enacted the laser shields. Being on the point, it was his role to protect the pair while Dog concentrated on the target.

Haggerty gave a self-satisfied grin as they penetrated the shell of Sua's long-range defense weapons without being fired upon. They were in time; the EAs hadn't discovered how to operate the station yet.

A sudden blinding flash of an anti-air rocket off his left wing wiped the smile away. He led Dog through two pre-planned evasive maneuvers, managing to avoid more rockets as their approach brought them into point defense range.

Then space lit up as the EAs unloaded everything. The laser shield burned as they started their bombing run. The pair danced in space, juking left and right, spiraling to avoid the station's wall of defense. Suddenly, a bright orange flash off his right side filled space, and the titanium shell of Haggerty's spacecraft rang with the staccato drumming of debris.

Dog was hit.

Haggerty had no time to mourn. The bombing role was his now, and a solo run required an immediate change of flight plan. Concentration on the job at hand crowded out any thoughts of Dog.

Space never seemed so small. There was flak everywhere. Laser fire, rockets. Haggerty's instincts took over. He twisted and turned, swooping between energy beams and gravity mines.

Ten seconds from the drop, he ducked low on the station—so low that Sua's external features blurred. It was a high-risk approach, but it nullified the station's defensive systems and it was a risk he was willing to take.

He dropped on target and two torpedoes impacted Sua's shell with deadly accuracy. He pulled up to avoid the debris that would follow. His only view of the explosion was its reflection off his bomber's skin. Moments later, huge chunks of the station flew through the vacuum and past his ship.

Then he was hit.

Crumbling metal shrieked in his ears. It was a sound that he had hoped never to hear, a sound that crawled up his spine and made him grind his teeth.

High-g acceleration threw Haggerty against the restraints. His muscles stretched and tore; the capillaries in the eyes bloated, bursting in white heat. His helmet bounced against the cockpit wall and shattered in a spider-webbed pattern.

Then silence.

Haggerty's vision blurred and tunneled.

Whatever was left of his ship was drifting, spinning through space. The whole array of red warning lights flashed in unison, clear one moment, faded the next. He tried to concentrate on one—FUEL SYSTEM MALFUNCTION. But he could not force his mind to tell him what it meant.

He managed to drag his hand along the armrest and depress an emergency sensor pad. If it still worked, the beacon signal would let his position be known.

His thoughts slipped away and his body went limp.

* * *

The setting was familiar—a dusty Arizona campground just outside of the Painted Desert. He sat cross-legged with his back against a large rock, watching the shifting sunset. It was multi-colored and vivid, hanging in the sky like a massive quilt woven in a Havasupai reservation. First came brilliant yellows and oranges that blazed over half the sky before giving way to softer shades of lavender and violet. The clouds were high and feathered, their underbellies picking up fiery-thin wisps of neon greens and pinks, creating the appearance of an abstract, computer-enhanced photograph. Deep radial streaks of violet and indigo rose in thick columns, overpowering the scene and reminding Haggerty of a child's painting before allowing the blue-black curtain of the desert night to crawl across the sky and steal the evening.

He heard his father.

"Lights out in the hen house." The voice was soothing and slow. It crept through the dim of the dusk to cover him like a woolen blanket. In the wavering light of the campfire, he studied his father's face. Leathered folds and sun-beaten wrinkles creased forehead and cheeks, the skin of an archaeologist. There was a line for every excavation, a fold for every trip he had taken with his only boy.

"Tell me a story, Dad?" He heard the pleading in his childhood voice. It was a high voice, that of a gawky, underweight teen.

The elder Haggerty's eyes shone as he gave a silent nod.

"There was a God who ruled the sun and who named himself Taiowa. His people were the Hopi, whose name translated as 'Peaceful'."

Hag grew comfortable. His strongest memories of his father were cemented in tales of the Hopi's holy migrations, the cities of the Havasupai, and the battle songs of the Navajo and Apache. But, of all his father's stories, legends of the Hopi caused the greatest stirrings in his heart.

"Taiowa gave the people great powers in the form of ritual and ceremony.

"To these people he said, *You will live together in peace. Your rituals will hold great power until they are either used for evil or your faith is abandoned.* Three times Taiowa created the world. Each time, the people began great wars, and he was forced to destroy his creation. The first world was destroyed by fire, the second by ice, and the third by water. Finally, when the survivors emerged into the fourth world, he said to them, *Each clan will leave this land to travel a solitary path. By this, you will learn that the tribe can remain strong only if the power of all rituals is combined.*

"So the tribes of the Hopi were split and lived nomadic lives as they followed their chosen trails for the next millennia.

"One by one, the clans returned to the holy land at the intersection of the paths, here in the Painted Desert. At first, their meetings brought great joy and they lived in peace. But over time, the lessons of their migrations died out and they began to war both with their own race and with other peoples. Weakened by these battles, they were crowded out of their land by the Navajo Nation. Taiowa, upset at their loss of faith, took back many of his rituals and left his people to dwindle to a pitiful few who still held faith."

The young Hag asked a question. "So, was the coming of the Navajo the end of the Hopi fourth world?"

The old archaeologist gave a cracked smile.

"Some say so, son. But I don't believe it. Petroglyphs across Arizona speak of a grislier prophecy. They tell of desolation so great that neither Hopi nor any other can live. No, I believe the fourth world has yet to close. Given today's environment, an indiscriminate plague or blanket of radiation will most likely mark its end.

"The point of the tale is, the Hopi lost their power because they lost themselves. They lost their inner direction and their faith in the Gods that defined them. To the few who held fast to their honor, who understood their part in the universe, the door to the fifth world—ever-lasting life—was left open." His father paused and spit into the dying campfire. His spittle gave a soft sizzle as it boiled into the arid night.

"There's something else."

Haggerty gazed at his father. "What?"

"Something I haven't told you before, son. Something I wanted you to be old enough to understand before you heard. Your great-grandfather was a Hopi."

"You mean I have Indian blood?"

"Yes." The word dangled in the nighttime like a fish hanging from the end of a line, twisting and turning, yearning to slip off into the darkness, but held firmly on the barb of his father's hook. "Don't lose your faith, son. You'll be judged by a higher power than we'll ever know."

* * *

He heard voices first. Unintelligible voices that spoke with urgent tones. Haggerty opened his eyes.

"Dad?"

His voice was coarse from dehydration. He watched as blue-smocked orderlies rushed from table to table distributing medicine and first aid in frantic doses. A young man moved to his side and checked a chart hanging from the arm of his bed. It gave a loud clatter as he replaced it.

"Where am I?"

The orderly gave a short double-take and returned the half-step he had moved.

"Haggerty's awake," he called out before turning his attention to him. "You're in the triage ward on the *UMS Devoted*. It's an honor to serve with you, sir. You're a hero." The orderly reached across the bed and replaced the cold cloth that Haggerty suddenly realized had been draping his forehead. The words brought the mission back to him.

"Anyone would have done it," was all he could manage. His head hurt when he talked.

"Just like a space jock. Loud as hell when there's nothing to prove and quiet as a mouse when there's reason to holler."

"How many dead?"

The young man's face clouded. "Heavy casualties, sir. I can't say the number offhand, but despite your efforts, the EAs managed to pretty much destroy the station."

"Huh?" It was as intelligent a reply as he could manage through the pain in his neck and the mist in his head.

"I'm not supposed to tell anyone of the casualties, but I think you're a special case." He bent and whispered into Haggerty's ear. "They got the President too."

"Who?"

"You heard me right. The President was on board. The God damned EAs killed the President."

Haggerty's mind raced through the fog. The General hadn't said anything about the Union's leader being aboard during the brief.

"You were the only unit in position to fight back. Hell, I apologize for babbling, I'm sure you already knew that. At least you got the bastards. Must have been a close-in kill. From what I hear, there's not a piece of their strike craft large enough to identify."

The kid gave Haggerty's shoulder a shake and moved off to check on another table.

* * *

Twenty-seven years of isolation will change a man.

Haggerty stood on an adobe platform in the middle of the Arizona desert and contemplated his life. He was older, now. His face was as marked as his father's had been, his full head of dark hair a distant memory.

He scanned the horizon, looking for a pinpoint of light. There it was—high in the sky, a brilliant marble tracing an arcing path through the atmosphere.

It was hard to believe it had all happened.

It was hard to believe that Ghostman, like an old-time sheriff, was coming to bring him to justice.

He breathed the desert air deeply and surveyed the dry, flat land that stretched to the horizon. Its desolation had saved it from the terror of Eurasia's nuclear onslaught. There was nothing to gain in destroying an already-devastated landscape whose population was minimal. Today, northern Arizona was an island surrounded by empty oceans of radioactive waste. Perhaps it was a holy land, a monument made by man's omission, given to the human race by God, or Allah, or maybe even Taiowa, through forethought and with certainty that the rest would be wasted.

He turned and retreated down the hatch and into the living quarters the empire had built while he was still a hero.

He went to his bedroom and pulled out his Space Force uniform. Survival in the sparseness of the Painted Desert had kept him trim. Despite the passage of time, the dark blue garments slid over his body with an old familiarity.

He had known that they would come back for him, of course. The empire was not comprised of people who got where they were by leaving loose ends exposed. And, under all definitions, he was surely that—a loose end like an ancient landmine, buried deep in the desert sand awaiting only pressure from an unknowing foot. It was surprising they had waited this long.

The communication had said that Captain Hubert Newlin, "Ghostman", was at the helm of the shuttlecraft. Haggerty did not let that twist of the knife go unnoticed. The assignment of Ghostman told him that his hopes were dim. There would be no aid from old friends or other unexpected sources.

For the first time in over twenty years, Haggerty placed a video chip in the recorder. Images rushed at him. Images of a dark-skinned, coal-haired bravo gazing back through the distance of time. Bright eyes and white teeth accentuated a lean, angular face. He was his father's boy. Tall. Strong. The uniform carried an array of decorations—the Seven Suns Cluster, Defender's Cross, and numerous small citations.

Originally, the empire had been content to isolate him in the vacuum of "retirement," locked away in his personal universe. They held a celebratory day in his honor and awarded him the

Union's highest commendation. Then they left him to live out his life on earth.

He glimpsed himself in the wall mirror and stopped to straighten the attire.

The uniform's creases remained sharp from the last time it was worn. Captain's silver braid looped across his shoulder in the style of his generation—elegant. He had never removed the medals. They hung, tarnished, like dead leaves clinging to a winter oak. The hat would never stay on in the gusting wind, so he decided against it and returned to the surface with his head exposed.

The shuttle had made its way through the atmosphere and now was a black dot hovering over the western horizon. He shaded his eyes and squinted as he searched for it. *A pilot's instincts never die,* Haggerty thought as he spotted the craft. Ghostman came for him out of the sun.

He stood motionless in the desert wind and watched the shuttle's approach.

The craft kicked up a cloud of dirt and sand as it set down two hundred meters from his doorstep. While the dust settled, a squad of MPs made its way out. Then Ghostman stepped forward and began walking toward him. The MPs fell in behind their superior officer in a loose formation. For a moment, Haggerty's calm eroded, and he fought back the leading edge of panic. There was still time to turn away, still time to dash into his chambers and make them kill him here rather than face the humiliation of a politically tainted war trial. His heart pounded against his breastbone and his nostrils flared with several unconscious breaths. The creatures that fluttered about his stomach and tied it in knots felt more like buzzards than butterflies.

The MPs stopped at Ghostman's signal, but Haggerty's old wingman continued forward until he was a pace and a half away. The wind blew his hair about, pushing it fore and aft in stiff waves. Haggerty looked through eyes rimmed with crow's feet. He inclined his head in greeting. Time had worn well on his friend.

It was Ghostman that broke the silence.

"Captain Haggerty." His voice was smooth and comfortable, textured like a favorite pair of pants. His face showed hollow anguish for a friend, an expression that gave Haggerty comfort.

"Captain Newlin," was Haggerty's simple reply.

"I'm here to bring you back to the Capitol for trial."

Years ago, after realizing that this day was certain to come, Haggerty had wondered what pretext they would bring with them. What storyline would be concocted to support his arrest? He could never come up with anything convincing enough to kill him without a trial—apparently, neither could the empire. "What do they have on me, sir?"

"It's bad." Newlin shook his head; he was graying at the temples. "The charge is treason. Something about killing the President." Ghostman gave Haggerty a straight, soulful stare before motioning the MPs to encircle him.

Two moved to place restraints over his hands.

He did not resist.

Haggerty smiled. It was a saccharine-sweet, all-knowing expression. "I expect it's a complete package. Original flight plans, video playbacks, unstable psychiatric background report...."

"All of those and more, Captain."

Haggerty hesitated before responding. During the pause, the MPs began to escort him back toward the shuttlecraft. Ghostman kept pace beside him in silence.

"What's the formal story, Ghost? Can you tell me that much?"

"I suppose it can't hurt anything. You'll get it all within the week anyway." He pursed his lips and continued. "You were assigned to a routine sentry pattern in defense of the President's visit to Space Station Sua. The vids show your ship peeled off the formation and somehow managed to evade point defenses before deploying torpedoes right down the chute." Ghostman paused and cocked his head, looking at his old friend.

Haggerty nodded and remained silent.

They walked him back to the shuttle and deposited him in a small holding bin. After the thirty-minute sortie back to the cruiser, he found himself quartered in a small, barren chamber with little but a bed, a hard-backed chair, and facilities. It would be a long trip. He settled in and took a nap.

* * *

He awoke to the pressure of a hand on his chest. It was a firm hand with light age spots and well-kept nails. His eyes followed a blue-clad arm back to find Captain Newlin seated in the chair.

"Ghostman," he said in a voice choked from sleep.

"Night Hag, good to see you, my friend." Without the platoon of MPs about, the formality of their last meeting was now absent.

"It has been a long time."

"Twenty-five years," Newlin sighed.

"Twenty-seven and a half." Haggerty was unable to keep a tinge of spite out of his voice as he corrected his wingman.

Silence hung stale in the air for a moment. Haggerty sat up, swung his feet over the edge of the bed, and got straight to the point. "What made me want to do it?"

"Fatigue. Too many missions without a break. Your service record is impressive for such a short career. The Space Force is funding a review of combat leave policy based on your case." Ghostman's voice was thick.

They would paint him as psychotic. Even though he had prepared himself for this approach, its reality hit hard. "What made them realize their history books were wrong?"

Ghostman leaned closer to his old friend. Haggerty thought he could see the question in his eyes. "Space debris. Pieces of the station's main computer were recently found floating around one of Jupiter's moons. They claim the planet's magnetic field kept the wreckage hidden from sensors until an exploratory mission picked it up. They have video chips showing your ship in action, Hag. Retrieved from the central memory unit. The rest they pulled together from intensive studies of old documentation."

The face of his father came back from the dream. It carried a serene countenance.

"I did it, Ghost. I killed the President. That's all you need to know."

"No," Ghostman replied with an even-toned voice. "I knew you better than anyone. Probably better than you knew yourself. We lived through flight school together. The day I became your wingman was my proudest as a pilot. I refuse to believe you went traitor or haywire." The words came with such conviction there could be no argument as to their validity.

Haggerty saw his friend through eyes twenty-seven years younger. Between them, the empire's story did not play, and he knew it. "All right. I'll tell you my version, but with the condition that you keep your lips sealed. No reason to ruin two lives instead of one."

Ghostman inclined his head slightly and looked through arched eyebrows.

"I'll agree with the condition as long as the situation is as cut and dried as you make it sound. Fair enough?"

"No. That's not good enough, Ghost. This is important. You'll keep it quiet, or you won't hear it."

Ghostman was silent for a moment. "I understand. I had forgotten how stubborn you were once your mind was set."

Haggerty took a deep breath. After waiting for this opportunity, he was unsure of how to start.

"Dog Cunningham and I were called into the briefing room. I knew it was something big when it was just the two of us and the General," Haggerty started. He proceeded to spend the next fifteen minutes detailing the events that had led to his attack on Sua.

Adrenalin rose in his system as he relived the event. He stood up and paced across the little room—his voice tightening with every step.

"I'll tell you one thing, Ghost. It was a bitch getting through the point lasers. It was the hairiest flying I ever did. Just incredible. Green and red flashes came from everywhere, I swear to God it was Christmas. I remember thinking that we were wrong about how long the EAs had held the station. They shouldn't have been this prepared. Dog was taken out. But I got in so close I could almost read the serial numbers on the solar tiles. I had seen all the construction specs, so the target definition was easy. I dropped right on.

"My ship was torn up. There wasn't much left but the cockpit and backup life support systems— thank goodness for redundant designs. All I remember is floating through space, rotating endlessly. I think one of the side-pod gravity drives was still functional; I must have seen the sun cross the window a hundred thousand times before I lost consciousness.

"When I woke up, I was being attended to on a cruiser. Superficial wounds mostly. A concussion from the g-force of the break-up was the worst of it. It was there that I figured out the Eurasian Space Force hadn't been within a light week of Sua. I knew something was going on, but everything was happening too fast. I didn't have time to comprehend it all.

"Being picked up by the cruiser probably saved my life twice. Beyond purely snatching me out of the vacuum, enough people recognized me in that cruiser's sick bay to make it difficult for anyone to make me disappear later—especially since the Union started broadcasting information about an EA attack on Sua. Everyone seemed to know who I was, but nobody knew the reality of what I had been doing out there. They just assumed I had been fighting the onslaught and I became a hero.

"I blew some plans when I turned up alive. The General came by, and we talked. He was nervous at first, but after he realized I hadn't told anyone about the details of our mission he relaxed. We talked it through for weeks before agreeing on my retirement. They gave me my choice of where I wanted to live and offered to build me a home—as long as it was a very long way from any other civilization.

"I think he about crapped his pants when I told him I wanted to go back to earth! The war had continued during our discussions, and the place was desolate. No one else would be living there—or would even want to for quite a while. The Arizona desert was among the few inhabitable areas left. But it was home to me, and I agreed to it. The General was so happy I thought he was going to kiss me.

"You know the official slant. They filled every news vid with press releases. *George Haggerty the war hero. George Haggerty, the pilot who almost sacrificed it all to fend off Eurasia's attack on the President. George Haggerty, the man whose courage was rewarded with his choice of retirement houses*—at least the last was close to the truth. And it worked. The public was infuriated by the attack. The new president re-dedicated the nation to victory. No tactic was considered unacceptable from that point on—even the destruction of the earth. After all, we could live in space and Eurasia wasn't ready for that, yet."

Ghostman finally intervened. "The best of all worlds."

Haggerty took a deep breath and sat down on the hard cot. "Yes."

Ghostman's face drew down as if in deep thought. He rubbed his temples between his index finger and thumb. "So, the president was assassinated in a military coup?"

"You got it."

"That doesn't make any sense, Hag. Why?"

Haggerty breathed deeply. "After twenty-seven years of thinking it through, I think I've about got it pieced together right. Think about it. At the start of the war, both sides rode high tides of patriotism. We had our usual national bravado, and our outright refusal to share knowledge gained from building Sua station brought the Eurasian countries together against a common enemy. But by the time of the mission, the gruesome casualties of space war had turned enthusiasm sour. The war was not winnable without a strong basis of public support. And that was dwindling. A dramatic prodding of the masses was needed. What better than having the enemy assassinate our figurehead?"

"Interesting story, Hag. But if it's true, why come after you now? After all, it's been a quarter of a century since the incident."

"I've come up with several possible reasons, but I may never know for sure," Haggerty replied. "Maybe some of the key participants of the charade died off and I became the only living link to the truth. The President has to know about the scenario. Maybe he finally found it objectionable to have a loose end out there waiting to be found. Or maybe the General has finally grown tired of worrying about me. Given that I stayed healthy, I might live another thirty years. By that time, people might even return to resettle parts of the earth. Hell, maybe they really did find Sua's main computer. The real video chips could easily back their story. I figured it would come back to me sooner or later."

Ghostman's eyes took on a far-away quality. "General Richard is an Admiral now—he's quite influential."

Haggerty's reply was a silent nod.

"I still don't get it, Hag." It was Ghostman's turn to stand. He paced and scratched his head as he spoke. "Why did you accept retirement? Why not blow the whistle back then?"

"Come on, Ghost. I thought you said you knew me. I believed in the cause enough to agree to anything. Once I understood the situation, I helped create the stories that covered their tracks."

An awkward silence filled the time.

"How will you plead?" Ghostman finally said.

"Guilty, of course." Hag's response carried no hesitation.

Ghostman's face registered shock. "Why? Why not tell your side?"

Haggerty's laughter filled the little room.

"Even if I had the desire to contest it, there is not a shred of evidence to back up my version of the incident. With all the documentation available, I would come out looking like some crazy lunatic who dreamed up wild, off-the-wall allegations to save his own butt. I've lived the last couple of decades like a hermit and I'm sure that the empire's psychologists could make a strong case by themselves. Maybe they would even argue that the cells of my brain had deteriorated through exposure to radioactive waste. I would be a poor, pathetic creature, fit only to be pitied. There is no chance I could win."

Haggerty halted for a moment and took a deep breath.

"I don't want to fight the empire, though. I believed in what we were doing with all my heart. I did it, Ghost. And even though you say you know me better, I would have done it even had I known the truth of the mission. But twenty-seven years of reflection let me know I was wrong. Not merely the idea of killing the president. The whole thing. We destroyed our world, Ghost—brought it to its knees and forced our people to live in tin cans floating around the universe."

A heavy silence filled the room before Haggerty continued in a tone laced with equal parts of pride and conviction. "The world was filled with factions. Now, even though we're scattered across the solar system, at least all humans live under one constitution. What good can I bring with this revelation?"

Ghostman's face showed deep creases. "You were operating under false knowledge fed to you by a superior officer. He is the one who should be held responsible."

"Ah...then I am innocent because I was an ignorant pawn whose only crime is blindly following orders?"

"Exactly."

Haggerty shook his head slowly. "I fought the war to create a democratic galaxy. I thought I had killed an entire space station of Eurasian soldiers toward that goal. Before that, I performed worse missions—you did, too, Ghostman. I will not try to tear down what's left of the world by stabbing at a hidden sore."

There was a moment of silence while Hag searched for words. His mind snapped to the dream he had experienced while floating through space, and a distant look crossed his face before he proceeded. "My father spent a lot of time telling me Native legends. One of those carried the lesson that the spearhead only travels where a man tosses it. Perhaps, in this case, I *was* simply a spearhead, and if there *was* any reasonable evidence to back my story, I could be absolved of legal guilt for this crime. Or, at the very least, given a reduced sentence."

He breathed deeply to clear his thoughts before continuing.

"But his most important stories told me that life is not a game where a man can switch sides at will. Clans who did not retain their faith lost their powers and could not cross over to the next world. Our religions have similar if less stringent restraints. I decided to plead guilty the day that I volunteered for the Space Force. If I am not guilty of the crime I'm charged with, I'm certainly guilty of a greater one. Because, in this case, the spearhead could make his own decisions. I chose to fly the mission. My decision. I'll live—or die—with it. I doubt my soul would be absolved of all repercussions for the mere fact that I was unaware of who died by my torpedo, or that they may have been the 'wrong' people. I will find that out shortly, I suppose. This way, I end my life with some shred of dignity."

Ghostman leaned against the wall of his cell. "Don't you feel even a little angry?"

"Only that the General did not trust me enough to tell the truth before I took the assignment," Hag answered with slow consideration. "Put yourself in my place, Ghostman. Think about it. I knew you as well as you knew me. You would have flown it too."

* * *

The courtroom where George Haggerty was convicted and sentenced was embedded deep in the chambers of the space ring orbiting Mars colony

Sandia. He was executed on the planet below and buried with two secrets.

One, he had told only his last friend. That he had flown a mission without knowing the real target and, in doing so, had changed the universe forever.

The other was a kernel hidden in his genes.

His father had passed down legends while they studied together in the deserts of southwestern America. And one hot evening in the Painted Desert, he had told Haggerty of his Indian heritage.

Yet, his father had not known the last grain of truth, either.

So, he could not have explained that when the gravediggers of Mars colony Sandia buried George "Night Hag" Haggerty, they entombed the last human being whose veins carried any trace of the blood of the Hopi.

As they lowered his body into the red clay of the Martian soil, the gates to another world opened. Bright lights, brilliant and dazzling, poured through the crack, enveloping Haggerty's soul and beckoning him to enter.

None of the grave diggers or other attendants paid it any heed or, indeed, even saw it. For the fifth world was only for the honorable. And only for the race who named themselves Peaceful.

And they were not of the chosen.

Night School

"I have Rebel-trace at seventy-five east. Repeat, Rebel-trace at seventy-five east. Request pincher action." The voice of the company leader sounded distant in Stoner's earpiece. He queried his display and accessed the caller's location.

"Roger, Maven. Pincher enroute."

He worked his way down Atherton High's south wing in stealthy runs of ten and twenty meters, crouching momentarily at each shadow-black classroom recess. A ghost-thin sheen of greenish neon sprang from exit signs that hung along the ceiling like distance markers for hallway hunters. Adrenalin scrubbed his veins and a familiar metallic flavor resonated on his tongue. The taste was strong tonight, pungent, lingering like the smell of gasoline and motor oil that used to hang on his grandfather's hands and clothes.

Was it like this the night that David died?

He chased the thought of his brother away and activated his radio. "Estimated arrival at observation point twelve in five minutes, Maven." His voice was a mere whisper.

"Roger. We are on hold."

Seizure and control of observation point twelve was Crimson company's first objective. It served as Atherton High School's communication hub, housing an integrated computer facility, outside phone lines, and an antique intercom system.

Stoner looked to his visor's lower right quadrant and glimpsed the timer. He could take a shortcut and cross the grassy lawn rather than loop through the network of hallways.

"Maven, I'm working to reduce that last estimate. Will report when ready."

"Roger."

He hustled to the next alcove and examined the classroom door. Like the rest, its glass panels were covered with emblems painted in thick oils. Traces of the day's heat lingered on each pane, registering wraith-thin images on Stoner's visor. It was Atherton tradition to allow seniors to decorate the doors in whatever fashion they desired — within limits. Briefly, Stoner wondered how many pages of Atherton's history he would find if a can of turpentine were handy. And he wondered if one of those pages would depict a crimson-clad boy lying in a pool of his own blood.

He reached for the knob. It felt cold through the skin-tight material of his uniform. Once he had turned the knob full to the stop, he readied himself and pushed through.

It was a mistake. A single, bare bulb glowed with hot radiance from a corner of the classroom. With his visor set on maximum infra-red, Stoner's eyes were bathed in an intense pool of greenish-white light. He groaned and brought his hands to his head; it took several seconds to disengage the helmet's battery power and another to slide the visor up. Huge orange blobs hung in the air, expanding and contracting in an odd, psychedelic cadence. Finally, from across the room, Stoner made out a small, pale face.

The kid wore a maroon T-shirt and a ragged pair of gold shorts — Atherton's colors. A mop of red hair capped a face covered by mottled patches of freckles. He stood with his back against the wall and his hands drawn up under his chin. A computer monitor and keyboard sat on the table beside him, and a swivel chair stood between him and Stoner. The kid had to be a first-year or advanced middle school. He posed no threat.

Stoner realized how lucky he was. He realized he could have come upon a Rebel military boy. In which case, he would be dead now. For a moment, Stoner remembered the look on his mother's face when the school representative reported David's death. He remembered the way her skin blanched and her hands shook. He remembered that same look when he had informed her of his decision to follow in David's footsteps and join Central's Crimson Company. And he remembered the only words that she had managed before leaving the room. *Make us proud of you.*

"Son, you are in the wrong place at the wrong time," Stoner said as his hand snaked to his utility belt. His grasp molded around the hard curve of a sturdy throwing knife.

The child stammered. "Don't hurt me — I'm just studying. I didn't mean no harm. I won't tell on you."

Civilian or not, the boy should be silenced. It would do no good to leave a witness to alert Rebel sentries. But Stoner remembered spending long nights of his own in Central's computer center. His single-minded dedication to academics was legendary. Sometimes he did not sleep at all. "Stoner's become a RAM chip," his friends would jest as they partied in their dorm rooms. Higher mathematics, computer technology, the physical sciences, and of course, military history and tactics had been his summer companions before and after his first year.

Stoner looked at the kid. The boy almost trembled with fright, just like Stoner himself would have reacted before David taught him how to take control of situations. The thought made him pause. He felt a kinship; he couldn't bring himself to kill the boy.

"What's your name?" he finally asked.

"Stanley." The boy's voice trembled slightly with the reply.

Stoner did not find the name adequate and immediately shortened it. "Well, Stan, what are you doing here?"

"Just st-studying for my calculus project. What are you doing here?"

The kid was fresh. He didn't even know the game. "We're gonna take your school — welcome to Central High," he said with a sarcastic drawl.

While Stanley mulled the statement, Stoner rubbed his eyes and gazed around the room. Schools aren't much different, he thought. Rows of neatly aligned tables sat silently awaiting tomorrow's rush of activity. Posters of historical figures filled one wall — Lincoln, Churchill, Kennedy, King, and Stephens. A porcelain whiteboard, filled with multi-colored scribbling, spanned another. Stoner recognized the scribbling. American History — they were covering one of his favorite topics, Neil Armstrong's first steps on the moon. Stoner's ultimate dream was to be on one of the first Martian expeditions. They couldn't be more than ten years away, and with enough work, he would make this dream a reality. He had already written to NASA for suggestions as to how best to prepare for the life of an astronaut. It was their response that pushed Stoner's decision to join Crimson Company.

"Why?"

"What's that?" Stoner said as he snapped out of his observations.

"Why do you want our school?"

The commando's smile was immediate. "We'll use it as an operations outpost. From here we can install scanners that will reach three other schools."

Stanley seemed shocked. "You don't even want our teachers?"

Stoner gave another brief smile and remembered his naive understanding of High School politics.

"Oh, we'll probably use them. I know you've got a social lit guy who's supposed to be pretty good and a physicist who ranks in the state's top fifty. But Atherton's real value is its strategic location."

"You'll take Atherton merely because then your army will have a better scouting position?"

Stoner pursed his lips and nodded. "With access to bigger schools, we can plan actions to pull the best resources from them, ensure our students are provided the best education possible, and enable us to become better citizens." He spoke with a tone that comes from practiced repetition.

"What will happen to Atherton's students?"

"You'll be absorbed into the Central coalition. You'll fit behind our originals, of course. We wouldn't deprive any of our kids of a top-flight education just because we assimilated another school. But the cream of Atherton's academic minds will still rise to the top."

He paused to point to the bright blue computer screen filled with an archaic programming language, just what one would expect of a kid. Stoner scanned the code on the screen. It was an integrating subroutine that modeled a feedback loop. He smiled. This was the type of project that he used to love working on with David. Small routines, trivial games to others, but after enough years these little projects could be linked and combined, molded into larger systems capable of performing great tasks.

"Someone like yourself will do just fine. Keep playing with this stuff and you might even get to work on the super-computer in two years."

"But Atherton is number three in the state in aggregate graduation scores," Stanley said. "Why draw us down just to make it possible for you to get stronger? Doesn't that defeat the purpose?"

Stoner frowned. This sounded like the beginning of peacenik speeches he had heard before. "Stan, I'm not here to argue social issues," he snapped. He reached up to turn his helmet's power back on. His visor flipped down and fell into place with an authoritative click.

But Stanley would not let up.

"Seriously, don't you think this approach sub-optimizes society? Why can't we work something out where we could share resources and use each other's talents and strengths so that both of our schools could ensure their students get the best education and enable us to become better citizens?"

Stoner's temples constricted. He checked the operations timer. This little shortcut had cost him five minutes and he was sure Maven would be getting antsy by now. He looked at Stan. The boy's body coursed with the conviction of his speech. Inside his helmet, Stoner smirked. Yes, Stan should be killed to ensure mission integrity, but Stoner remembered a time that he was no better off than the boy. He remembered the hours that David had spent with him, teaching him the ropes. And when he remembered these images, Stoner knew he wouldn't kill Stan. Instead, he would take him under his wing, tutor him, he would be just like David.

While the last of these thoughts ran through his mind, Stoner walked to the computer and yanked out the communication port. This way Stan couldn't raise a stink in enough time to make a difference.

"Stan, you talk an interesting game. Stay here for a few minutes. I'll come back when it's all over. You've got potential — a man with your conviction stands a fair chance of accomplishing anything he wants. I'll look after you, too. You'll make out just fine."

He went to the window that opened out onto Atherton's campus lawn. He would have to sprint to avoid detection. But no one would be expecting this tactic and there were enough trees to provide the cover necessary to break the maneuver into smaller runs.

As he leaped out the window, a bolt of energy caught him in the back and left him sprawling, lifelessly, on the grassy lawn.

* * *

Stanley lifted his finger from the keyboard. Thin smoke rose from the monitor and filled the room with the bitter scent of ozone.

The program worked! Even though it was just the initial prototype, and even though all his teachers had told him that a monitor couldn't serve as a projection device, it had worked!

He was ecstatic. With this weapon, Atherton would rule the district. Yes, the discharge system would have to be modified — it wouldn't do to require the replacement of a monitor every time the weapon was used — and the carrier virus needed to be perfected. But once he introduced it to the school system's network, Atherton Army would have a cache of secret weapons at any school in the state. He pulled a headset from behind the screen and broadcast an alert.

Stanley's mother would be so proud.

A Corner of the Mind

How many times have you heard the saying: "If the walls had ears and could talk, what tales they would tell"? Well, they do, and I'm one. So let me tell *you* about the young boy who often does time here in one of *my* corners.

Jack is a good-natured kid whose desires run in the same vein as those of every other youngster who ever existed—a sprint through Alpha deck's corridors at break-neck speed, a chance to one-up his acquaintances at holo-ball, and maybe a quick ice cream cone before bedtime.

But space travel is a tough life for a pre-teen.

Especially if that pre-teen happens to be the only son of the ship's Chief Security Officer. Jack's dad is a space cop of the highest order. He's a brute of a man, who stands nearly two meters tall and reeks of military regimentation, a man whose gung-ho attitude would be almost bearable if this ship weren't just a mid-class freighter.

Jack's mother was lost before they came aboard. Vacuum accident, they say, but the ship's records are fuzzy on the incident.

The boy has been cooped up here ever since.

Ten or twelve other children his age are aboard, but he has yet to be accepted into that clique. Of course, Jack has never gone out of his way to be one of the crowd, either. Yes, he plays with them, and yes, he often wins. But there is something different about him. He plays games that the other children can't. Until recently, only I had seen him play when he was alone. Only I could bear testimony to the countless mind twisters he worked, the computer wizardry he performed, or the intricate puzzles he created and solved. Truly, he is not like the rest. His imagination is a marvel to behold. Call it telepathy, call it reading auras, call it what you will. Jack sees things others can't.

And he can create.

Anyway, I felt terrible for the child. Here it was, a shade over a week until the ship's scheduled Christmas festival. The boy was excited. Who wouldn't be? As time drew near, all his friends could talk about was Santa Claus and toys, and Rudolph the Red-nosed Rocket. Jack woke up that morning sporting the radiant smile that only a child can muster. He caught his father right in the act of wrapping his Christmas presents.

Captain Horner had been on duty all night and I can assure you he was tired. However, that's a lame excuse for blowing up at his only son and sending him to that dingy little corner of his room, merely because the boy happened to catch him in the act of playing Santa.

Jack's face darkened as he sat on the stool, and he bit his lower lip. He glanced over his shoulder while his father put the presents under the tree.

"I'm taking a shower," Captain Horner said when he was finished. "Don't move till I'm back."

So Jack sat in the corner and thought.

And when Jack thinks, things happen.

The first image he created was his mother. She was tall and lanky with shoulder-length black hair and an almond-shaped face. She leaned over Jack and laid her hand gently against his cheek, all the while telling him how proud she was of him for doing so well in school. She kissed his forehead and stood up straight before the image dissolved.

I must admit to being surprised when the next image turned out to be of Jack's father. I can't remember Jack ever including his father in his games before. I almost didn't recognize the man. The captain was decked out in hiking gear—flannel shirt, denim pants, brown leather boots—and toting a heavy backpack. He looked healthy and strong, invigorated. His eyes sparkled and he was quick to take on a smile. Jack, younger in this scene by at least three years, walked behind his father, wearing a similar style of clothing but carrying a smaller pack. A forest enclosed them, offering only a thin path leading forward.

I think it important to note that Jack does not usually conjure images that contain himself, either. Through this fact, I came to think these last two shots were real scenes from his past, memories he held down deep in his heart.

Jack's father dropped to one knee. He beckoned Jack closer and wrapped his arm around the boy as he drew near. Jack's gaze followed his father's as he pointed to a chipmunk that dashed from tree to tree. Jack smiled.

Then that image disappeared, and a new scenario grew.

This time, the mood was somber. There was soft music in the background and people milled around, dressed in formal attire, and speaking in quiet voices. A small, decorative casket sat on a pedestal along the far wall—the kind of casket that is displayed when the body remains unrecovered. Captain Horner materialized in the middle of the room. His face was drawn and haggard, his hands clasped behind his back and his gaze lowered. Another man stood next to the captain, with his hand on his shoulder.

"I should have saved her," Jack's father said.

"You know you would never have made it back," the man said. "And you have a boy to worry about."

"*I* sent her out there. *I'm* the one who found the anomaly, and *I'm* the one who decided to study it."

"Marie was the mission specialist, John. And a damned good pilot. Everyone knows she was the best choice."

"I checked out the surveying pod myself," Captain Horner replied. "Somehow, I missed something."

"Don't kick yourself, John. You didn't miss anything, and you know it. The pod was clean. Post-ops didn't find anything wrong."

"Then how do you explain what happened? Why were communications interrupted? Why did the cabin lose pressure? How do you explain that Marie is gone?"

Soft organ music filled the silence.

"I should have gone out there."

"You can't blame yourself, John."

"Yes." Jack's father said, his jaw clenching as he swallowed hard. "Yes, I can."

The image vanished, and Jack stared with wide-eyed bewilderment at the spot where his father had stood. Until this moment, I don't think he realized how much his father blamed himself for his mother's death.

Jack seemed to think for a moment, then closed his eyes and began conjuring. This wasn't his usual creative process. This time his hands and body swayed with effort. His eyes closed and small beads of sweat suddenly appeared on his forehead.

Another image formed—his mother seated in a cramped cockpit. She stared at the controls, furrows creasing her forehead, her lips drawn into a tight line. Lights from the panel pulsed on and off, casting alternating blotches of red and green over her face. Her fingertips brushed lightly over buttons and touchscreens, but nothing happened.

She pushed the communications control and spoke.

"I don't know if you can hear me, Central, but everything's dead here. I'm going EVA to see what's up with the main power cell."

She pulled a spacesuit out of a small locker at her side and, despite the tight confines of the pod, managed to wriggle into it. The airlock mechanism still worked, and within a minute, she stepped into space.

As the door shut behind her, there was a flash of light. At first, I thought that the image had dissolved, but that was not the case.

Jack's mother had simply disappeared.

Jack held the image for a few moments longer, then let it slip away.

When it was gone, he finally noticed his father standing in the doorway, tears streaming down his face.

* * *

Christmas was postponed in the Horner household this year.

While the rest of the ship celebrated the holiday, Jack's father convinced the captain to return to the scene of the accident. It took two weeks to travel there, two weeks that the captain spent in intensive study. He reviewed videos, studied technical reports, and delved into advanced mathematics. He was a driven man, spending twenty hours a day poring over everything he could get his hands on. And all the while, Jack stayed by his side, using his talents to model complex, multi-dimensional geometries.

When they arrived, Captain Horner ordered a series of scans. Two days later, he found what he was looking for.

It was a small spatial rift—a pin-sized break in time.

Once this discovery circulated through the ship, the rest of the crew pitched in. Within a day, the entry point was found and Jack's mother was recovered.

She was thin and worn, but alive.

Sick Bay ran test after test, and even though Jack's mother had been missing for a full year, the doctors described her condition as being malnourished and dehydrated, as if she had been without food or water for only one week.

* * *

Three days later, when he heard that his wife was being released, Captain Horner commissioned himself chief swabby, and Jack his first assistant. They commenced scrubbing the floor, dusting the shelves, and vacuuming the carpet. Jack straightened up his room and put away his toys.

Both of them walked with a new attitude. Both whistled and sang to themselves.

Jack fell asleep that night with a dust rag in his hand. When he woke, he found his father had worked through the night. The table was set with their best dinnerware. The warm smells of fresh-baked Christmas pie and chicken soup—homemade, not the stuff from the regen facility—wafted through the air. Even the walls looked freshly scrubbed.

Late that afternoon, Jack's mother, still fragile, but walking under her own power, returned to their cabin. They ate a light meal—except for Jack, who ate like he would never get another opportunity. Jack told her about his last year in school. They swapped jokes. They laughed, sometimes for no reason at all. Jack had promised his father not to discuss his magic until his mother was stronger, so he kept that part a secret still.

And they opened presents.

The look of sheer excitement on Jack's face told me that this was the best holiday he had ever had.

As the evening grew into nighttime, Jack's mother and father moved to the couch to watch videos. Captain Horner sat tall, with his arm draped around her shoulder while she snuggled against his chest. They were both exhausted—he from staying up all night cleaning, and she from the exertion of coming home. They fell asleep, softly snoring.

After checking carefully on them, Jack went back to the table, picked up the Christmas pie, and walked to that same corner his father had confined him to before, pulling a stool along with him as he went. He sat down and rested back against the wall.

He closed his eyes for a moment and his whole body slumped. It looked as if the weight of the world had been lifted from his shoulders. Suddenly, Jack's mother disappeared.

Jack opened his eyes and looked at the Christmas pie, eyeing it hungrily. He quickly stuck his thumb into it. When he drew it out, a piece of fruit remained. He licked it off and looked at his father.

Concentration crossed his face again, and his mother reappeared.

Jack smiled. What was that? What did he say?

"Oh, what a good boy am I."

Intermission

Author's Note

We now come to the part of the book that makes me giddy.

As noted in my foreword, what follows is a story titled "The Train Robbery," which I wrote in high school, dressed up in the livery of a great novel, complete with faux blurbs, a Magic Marker cover, and an About the Author that rocks.

Then comes a few words about the letter I received from my teacher's assistant. Unfortunately, I have not been able to find the assistant to get permission to print his exact letter, so I'll be paraphrasing.

Alas, I hope I do him justice because reading his words all these years later prompted "The Hero," which is my rewrite of the story.

This may well have been my favorite story of all time when it comes to the writing part.

It was a total blast.

I debated what reading order I should lay these out in. Put the newer version first, and then the original? Vice versa? I saw valid reasons to do both.

In the end, I went with chronological order, mostly so that I could give my teachers' notes a bit of a guidepost to rest on.

If you'd rather read them in the opposite order, feel free.

With that, let's get started, shall we?

Bestseller
#1
The
Robbery
A novel
R Collins

A fantastic book! Collins is great!
—St. Louis Globe

Spellbinding. You forget everything until you've
finished the last page.
—New York Times

Ron Collins is one of the brightest young authors of
the decade.
—Playboy

The greatest thing I've ever seen.
—Time Magazine

[Modern Ron's Note: Please realize these are not
actual endorsements of these publications. I leave
them here as historical remnants of a teenage boy's
propensity for self-aggrandizement.]

*For me
(after all, I need the money)*

The Robbery

His strong blue eyes scanned the horizon. His old scuffed Stetson shaded his eyes and covered most of his short, sandy hair. The lines of many years were etched into his rough, bronzed face, and his lips were set in a straight, thin line.

Billy's eyes stopped.

He saw it.

The dense black smoke belched from the onrushing train.

"Let's go, men," he calmly said.

The seven trail-worn men gave spur to their horses and thundered off toward the far-off train.

* * *

Inside the train, the constant chugging was deafening. One of the wealthier passengers, Diamond Jim Walker, was trying to rest. But he knew he would never get to sleep with the methodic *clackety, clackety* of the metal wheels.

He rolled out of bed and sauntered to the tall, grimy window of his compact sardine can of a room.

He could see a small group of ragged men riding like the wind alongside the long, black snakelike machine on which he was a passenger. The steady rumbling of horse hooves could barely be heard over the screaming of the train.

As Jim watched, each determined man slithered into the black monster. A piercing scream overcame the noise of the train and horses. One careless man had lost his footing and slipped under the metallic wheels—gone for eternity.

A quick, penetrating rap on the door caught Jim's attention. He knew he was in trouble, and quickly began to hide his most expensive and cherished possessions.

"Open up," a gruff voice rasped through the paper-thin wooden door.

As Jim slowly cracked open the door, the incessant noise of the train flooded the room.

He looked the man over.

The bandit was over six feet tall, and well-built. His gleaming black gun knocked any notions of rebellion from Jim's head.

As the man shoved the door open, Jim silently moved to the corner of his dingy room. The bandit then proceeded to find all of Jim's hastily made hiding places.

* * *

Billy, the leader, had quickly made his way to the engineer's compartment. With his footsteps overwhelmed by the unyielding noise of the smoking, black engine, Billy was upon the engineer in a flash. As the engineer slid softly to the hard oak floor, Billy's hand went quickly to the brake lever.

The train came to a grinding, screeching halt.

* * *

Inside Jim's compartment, the bandit had been thrown off balance by the unexpected and sudden stop of the train. He went crashing headlong into the tiny bed.

Jim, taking full advantage of the desperate situation, grabbed an unlit lamp and sent it crashing into the young man's vulnerable head.

The frightened screams of women who were being robbed reverberated through the train as Jim's mind sprang into action. He shook his head and began to tie up the ragged, foul-smelling man.

He picked up his stolen items and grabbed the man's gun.

Stepping out into the corridor, he took careful aim upon two unsuspecting gunmen. The black dragon he held spat its deadly venom twice, and the two scraggly robbers fell with sickening thuds.

"There are three more to go," Jim quietly whispered to himself.

He didn't know how he was going to finish off all three of them. Trying to take them all at the same time was foolish. He decided he would try them one at a time.

He noticed the silence of the train.

Not a word had been uttered since the shots, and the only thing that could be heard was the probing wind, whistling through the now motionless train.

Two shots suddenly rang out.

Now alert, Jim slowly crept through the hallway, now filled with terrified screams. One of the invaders lay in the floor of the hall, a dark red fluid flowed from his chest.

"Only two more," he thought as he carefully peered around the corner of the tiny room.

A passenger was squirming on the floor in agony, a bullet through his shoulder.

After trying in vain to stop the man's bleeding, Jim went to find a doctor, clutching his protective gun to his side.

* * *

Stepping into the corridor, Jim came face-to-face with one of the marauding men. He was first struck by the man's age. He was only a green kid. Why, he couldn't be more than fifteen or sixteen. He wasn't even armed!

A brief scuffle erupted, during which Jim got clipped on the shin by the young man's sharp boots.

He quickly tied up the young bandit and attended to himself.

"Now the odds are even," he said to himself in a suddenly elated voice. "Only one more to go."

Jim felt much better with only one man between himself and personal glory. His mind whirled with the sweet thoughts of the money, friends, and publicity he would receive for stopping Billy "the

Kid." He was rich already, but he never felt like he had enough money to do whatever he wanted.

He thought of the newspaper headlines. *'Diamond' Jim Walker Personally Stops Train Robbery.* And he swooned over his newfound treasure.

* * *

A shot shattered the long silence, and the self-declared hero hit the floor with a solid thud. Billy steadily inched toward the fallen gladiator. A steady trickle of blood seeped from the gaping wound in Jim's back.

The hero ... was dead.

* * *

If you have read this story very carefully, you know there is a moral to Jim's actions.

That moral is: Don't count your chickens before they've hatched.

The Author

Ron Collins graduated from Manual High School in May 1979. Three weeks later this book came out, his first. In this first work, Collins shows the promise that his teachers, Mr. Sater and Mr. Abrams, said he had. We look forward to his next work of art.

Notes from Teachers

When I turned "The Train Robbery" in to my teacher in its full-blooded, novel-like form, I received a fantastic handwritten note back.

Technically, I had two teachers in that class, one being the primary English teacher, and the second his assistant. This means I received two notes, both handwritten (naturally). One was on the manuscript itself, the other on a separate slip of paper.

I recently found my "novel," complete with the notes.

The sight of them made me happy.

As I said earlier, however, despite heavy internet searching, reaching out to people I thought might know something, and even attempting to contact the school, I have not been able to get hold of my teacher to thank him and to obtain his permission to use his words directly. Hence I shall paraphrase.

The primary instructor noted that I had talent, and an ability to make other people see themselves.

I'm sure I didn't know what that meant back then, but I admit that simple acknowledgment rings through the years and fills me up. I like feeling like a kid again.

The assistant, however, went further, penning a full page of thoughts that, of course, praised the piece, but focused on the editing I'd been doing, and pointed out the use of various details and dialog as stronger.

He then said the following (which I will pull out as … ahem … fair use):

* * *

You do have a talent for writing, and I hope you will continue working on it – perhaps more than any other skill, in writing, practice is of utmost importance.

* * *

Is that awesome, or what?

If there's anything that rings true throughout my whole life as a writer, it's that practice is king. Writing is the only way to learn how to write. You can have mentors, and you can get feedback and everything else, but in the end, it all comes down to you and the page.

He then went on to complete the letter with the challenge that led to "The Hero."

You see, he suggested that I put the piece away for a while and come back to it fresh. He said I would be surprised by how much I would have grown.

Update from Ron

Well...I thought with a sly grin as I read that letter.

Is 45 years long enough?

Ha ha!

Indeed, it is!

So, of course, I couldn't help myself.

First though, in the extremely unlikely chance that my teacher reads this, let me address these lines to him.

* * *

Well, Mr. Sater, or is it Soter—I apologize for not remembering, and I can't quite decide from your signature. I set the story aside for a little longer than you suggested, but thanks to my Kickstarter backers, I've finally pulled out "The Train Robbery" and have taken a shot at doing a rewrite.

I hope you turn out to be right about my growth.

Either way, though, let me take a moment to tip my cap in your direction—wherever you happen to be. And also in Mr. Abrams's direction, though my internet search did reveal that we've lost him now. Looking back, being in your class was a formative moment for me.

So, thank you so very much, wherever you are.

Please know that I'm thinking good thoughts your way.

* * *

With that, here is my latest attempt at "The Train Robbery." I hope you enjoy it even half as much as I enjoyed writing it.

The Hero

Dismounting with the others, Billy the Kid scanned the hard-packed desert that sprawled endlessly in every direction. In the distance, the glint of train tracks blazed a bright gash into the blotchy brush.

Cactus and creosote, mostly.

The prickly aromas of hard vegetation rode the breeze. The taste of dirt was everywhere.

He ran the numbers through his head again. If they were true, they'd get him into the train's safe quicker than dynamite. If they were bad, well. Percy Haywood, the teller who'd given him the code, would be dead before tomorrow's sun showed.

On the horizon—south, toward Mexico—mesas rose up flat and square.

If they got far enough toward Arizona, and up north where Colorado lay, the mountains would grow sharp and cold. But here in New Mexico Territory, the land was flat, hot, and hard. The sky above was another span of nothing. Cloudless blue. Deeper than the watery gaze of Billy's eyes as they fixed on the tracks.

He was a slim man, Billy. Wiry.

He wore a stained, wide-brimmed sombrero to keep the sun from his skin, and a dark, dusty scarf that looped around his neck that gave equal value keeping the oven-forged winds from his cheeks as it did while keeping a person's gaze from catching his face.

He and the boys'd been in New Mexico Territory a while now. Almost made it straight a few years back. But, like everything else he'd done, being a ranching hand just didn't work out quite right. Then the whole thing in Lincoln County went bad and that was that. With Garrett and the rest gunning for him, Arizona and Navajo Country was sounding more promising every day.

First, though, there was the matter of funds.

The Santa Fe line ran at regular times, which made it easy to make plans. The lack of movement along the track now made Billy draw his chapped lips into a thin line, though. The train was late, and patience was not his greatest talent.

The boys, too, were restless.

They'd been full of chatter around the fire last night. Billy'd liked watching Sunny Boy, in particular. More than the rest because the kid was greener than green. Said he was fifteen, but Billy himself had been fifteen when his mama got sick, and his stepdad skipped out. Sunny Boy was no fifteen. Billy guessed him as thirteen, at best nearing fourteen.

Billy saw the kid's other tells, too.

This train would be Sunny Boy's first real job.

Billy'd brought this new group of riders together for this job because, other than Tommy, he didn't want anyone to recognize their association.

He liked Sunny Boy, though.

The kid had something fresh that made Billy want to watch him. If things went well, he'd bring the kid along just to look out for him.

Finally, a dark smudge of smoke blackened the sky. Bright sunlight glinted from the locomotive. The sound of its engine rumbled low.

Billy reset his sombrero.

"All right, boys," he said, taking his saddle again. "Let's get 'em."

Six trail-worn men gave spur to their dark horses and thundered off to intercept the train.

* * *

In his private compartment, "Diamond" Jim Walker tried to sleep off the effects of last night's activities. He needed to be fresh enough to start anew when the train arrived in Trinidad later. He had a girl there, too. And another in Dodge City, where he'd arrive the following evening.

Kansas City to Santa Fe, then back.

It was a trip he'd made four times since the line began to run. Often enough he'd begun to look for them as opportunities to let off steam and set his mind right for his time at home with his wife and three children.

Officially, he was sweeping funds from the banks again, gathering interest and claiming bond returns on the investments his business made backing mining operations. Unofficially, he was also providing varying amounts of motivation to ensure certain shop owners raised prices enough so they could pay for his protective services, which was good business on both ends of the candle.

Last night had been marvelous.

A rousing dance show, excellent cigars, and a good result at the faro table, which meant an extra spin upstairs.

The last had been on the house this time.

Now, however, Diamond Jim was not having fun. He had been up too long and drank too much. The pallet in the private sleeper was too hard, the car was so close to the locomotive that its godforsaken racket was deafening, and—given the direction of the wind—the window, which had to remain open if he didn't want to suffocate in the infernal heat, allowed great clouds of steam and smoke to billow in. The rattle of the train and the sway of the floor made his stomach flip worse than the ocean liner had during the trip he'd made to Cuba as a younger man.

Thank God he had been in no condition to eat breakfast this morning.

And even if all that had been fine, he would never get to sleep with the methodic *clackety, clackety* of the wheels over the track.

He would take it all up when the steward came round again. This car needed serious repairs.

Hearing a new sound, though, Jim's ears perked up.

Horses on the run.

He rolled out of bed to stagger to the window.

Yes. Horses.

Six.

Racing alongside the long snakelike column of the train, the steady gallop of their hooves on the hard plate of the desert drummed like heartbeats under the screaming machination of the train. Clouds of dust billowed behind the beasts. Manes and tails flailed as their riders drove them forward—each of those riders more ragged-looking than the last, and each with larceny in their eyes and pistols in their hands.

His chest constricted and his jaw clenched.

The closest rider guided his horse beside the car ahead, then the man grasped a handhold and jumped aboard. As the horse peeled away, another man—this one either more careless or less lucky—lost his footing while trying a similar maneuver and, with a piercing scream, slipped under the churning wheels—gone for eternity.

The sound of a door opening came from outside Jim's compartment. Heavy boots drummed on wooden planks.

He'd locked the bank receipts in the Santa Fe Line's safe in the front car, so barring dynamite, nothing would be lost.

Otherwise, he had no time to waste.

Jim grabbed his satchel and ripped open the compartment he'd used to stash cash from stops at Santa Fe and Las Vegas. Turning quickly, he shoved the money under the knotted mattress, then tried to smooth it. His personal roll would stay in his vest pocket—because if things went bad, losing gambling stakes wouldn't be devastating and sometimes giving a thief something to steal made that thief less likely to find other things.

He glanced to his boots, shoved against the bed. They were high-quality leather, but worn and dusty from his trip. Jim always dropped the watch fob his father had given him inside the left boot when he traveled.

The footsteps stopped outside his door.

Jim pulled the pearl-handled pistol from the holster he'd laid across the mattress before trying to nap. It was a small weapon, more suited for influencing prospective business partners at certain critical moments of negotiations than it was for gunfights with outlaws, but it made him feel better.

A penetrating rap came to his door.

"Open up," a gruff voice rasped.

"Coming," Jim called.

He grasped the gun firmly and cracked open the door. The incessant noise of the train filled the room, and the presence of the scoundrel filled the hallway.

Jim looked the man over.

The dark-haired bandit's face was young and dirt-lined, but he was over six feet tall and well-built. The edge to his gaze and the pitch-black hole of the gleaming gun barrel aimed at a spot right between Jim's eyeballs knocked any notions of rebellion from his mind.

"No need to make things messy now, is there?" the man said.

"No, fine sir, there is not," Jim replied, understanding from that introduction that this was simply business and that—if he were to just let bygones be bygones—no one was going to wind up bleeding to death on the floor of the Santa Fe train. Jim lowered his little pistol to the floor.

Slowly, as the man shoved the door open, Jim moved to the corner of the room to give the robber free passage. The man's odor followed him in, strong enough to bring Jim's nonexistent breakfast up to his throat. The man must have been in the desert since before Jim first left Kansas City.

The bandit then proceeded to find all of Jim's hastily made hiding places.

Including the toe of his left boot.

* * *

Billy made his way to the engineer's compartment knowing from the lack of gunfire at their approach that his man, Tommy, had been successful in boarding early and taking out the Pinkerton. The plan had been perfectly made and swiftly executed. The engineer had received no word of danger.

So now, with Billy's footsteps covered by the unyielding racket of the smoking, black engine, Billy was upon the engineer in a flash.

The man slid softly to the hard floor, and Billy leaned into the brake lever. The wheels locked and, slowly, the train came to a grinding, screeching halt.

Numbers ran through his head again. He flexed his fists and stretched his fingers.

It was time to get to work.

* * *

Inside Jim's compartment, the train's lurching stop threw the bandit off balance. The man crashed headlong into the tiny bed.

Jim, reacting instinctively, grabbed the heavy, unlit lamp on the stand beside the bed, and bashed it into the young man's vulnerable head. The metal frame crunched on impact. Crystal shattered. The bandit went limp.

The smell of blood mixed with the oil that now flowed from the lamp well, combining with the taste of hot dust to make something intensely intimate and feral.

Clutching what remained of the lamp, Jim found himself panting for breath.

The frightened screams from down the train's length broke the moment, though. Women being robbed.

The guy he'd clubbed appeared to be dead, but Jim wasn't taking chances. He grabbed a pair of bow ties and bound the foul-smelling man's hands behind his back. Then he picked up his stolen cash and key fob and grabbed the man's gun.

A Colt, he saw.

He hefted it and felt power coiled silently in his palm. The handle still radiated warmth from the man's grip. Opening the cartridge showed the gun was loaded. A solid weapon.

By his count, four more robbers were aboard.

With his money back, and with a real weapon at his disposal, Jim had no intention of letting any of these lice-infested gang of desert dogs take his livelihood again. Robbers were despicable. Cowards. To simply take a man's hard-earned money took a particularly cowardly kind of human.

The more he thought, the more he hated these men.

Strengthened with confidence, Jim first slipped on his boots and then stepped into the corridor—where he found another of the gunmen just stepping into the car.

Jim took quick aim, and the gun spat its deadly venom twice.

The scraggly robber fell, clearly dead this time.

"Two down. Three to go," Jim whispered wryly, feeling even stronger than before.

The gun felt warm.

He clenched his jaw and ground his teeth. Despite the numbers, he could do this. If he stayed lucky, he could drop them one at a time. And if he did, Jim had the sudden thought, he would become an instant hero. The idea gave him a thrill. He could easily imagine the sensation of walking into saloons and banks both with a swagger that would draw attention.

Taking care of this little problem would be good business.

The train was deathly silent now.

Not a word had been uttered since his shots.

The only sound was the probing wind, whistling with an unnerving tone through the motionless train.

He considered directions.

Gunmen had boarded the train to the rear—where the voices of the other passengers said they had been at work earlier. But the robbers had stopped the train, too, which meant at least one of them had been in the engine.

Two new shots rang out toward the back.

Stepping carefully into the next passenger car, Jim arrived at a grisly scene.

An invader lay face down in a pool of blood that was still spreading over the deck. A bullet had exited the man's back and broken the glass window. The splatter was so disquieting that he did his best to not look at it.

A man's voice groaned low and desperate coming from a compartment to his left.

Softer, feminine urgings rose.

"No, Carl. Don't you go and die now, you hear me? I'm not gonna let you die on me."

Still cautious, Jim edged around the doorjamb.

A man in a white shirt and a businessman's vest squirmed on the floor, gasping in agony as the shirt ran red, a bullet through his chest. The woman knelt with him. She pressed her crimson-coated hand over the wound as she continued to exhort him not to die. The man's blood ran over her sleeves.

A gun lay beside her.

"Did you shoot that man in the passageway?" Jim said, amazed at the idea of this fragile woman defending herself with such brutality.

"Don't just stand there," the woman commanded as her brown gaze fell on his. "Help me!"

He couldn't tell if the wound was going to be fatal or not, but it didn't look good.

"I'm not a doctor," he said with a sudden panic.

He didn't like not knowing what to do.

"Do I look like I care what you are? Be a man and do something!" She turned back to Carl. "I'm telling you, Carl Hinson. Don't you die on me."

"I'll see if I can find a sawbones," Jim said.

Which he certainly would do if he could manage it.

His heart was pumping hard now, though. His thoughts were coming together fast, and it seemed like time had no existence. The idea of saving a man's life while also breaking up a train robbery of this magnitude would make him even more of a true hero.

The Santa Fe Line would probably bring him up for a reward.

Senses raised, Jim went back to the hallway, stepping over the dead man and feeling a kinship with the Colt in his hand. "Two left," Jim thought.

In the corridor, Jim came face-to-face with another of the marauders.

"Are you good there, Frankie?" the robber said, his voice high and almost frail.

The kid was young.

And he wasn't armed.

His eyes were dark, and his skin said he was a mix of some kind. Probably Indian, but Jim never could see any difference between a native and a Mexican, and he wasn't prejudiced. Long as a man was good to work the mines and buy store wares, he didn't care one way or another.

The kid froze when he saw the body, though.

His gaze rose to Jim's and his jaw dropped.

"We don't need to be doing nothing messy, now, do we, kid?" Jim said, stealing the first bandit's sense of irony.

The boy was nervous, though. Skitty.

He pounced at Jim and a brief scuffle erupted, during which Jim got clipped on the shin. But Jim was bigger, and he quickly subdued the young bandit. "I don't wanna shoot you in cold blood," Jim grunted, holding the boy down. He crashed the gun handle across the boy's jaw twice and the kid went unconscious.

After tying him down, and attending to himself, Jim refigured the situation.

"Now the odds are even," he said. "Only one more to go."

Yes, he thought, feeling momentum grow.

One more and he was a true hero.

One more, and he was golden.

The last man would be where the safe was.

* * *

Billy passed through the coal tender to get to the postal car, which was secure because no passenger could get access at all. It held the mail, of course, but also the company's bank vault.

The sounds of shots distressed him, but it wasn't a surprise that the passengers didn't want to give up their cash and other lovelies so easily. This, too, was a reason he'd brought a fresh team for this job. They'd take their cut from the passengers they were being paid to distract while he bent to the task of emptying the safe, and if one or two got themselves shot along the way, that's how the cards fall.

If he worked fast enough, things would figure themselves out. And he had Tommy to look out for him, too.

He ran the numbers again.

It was time to find out if Mr. Haywood was going to live or die.

* * *

Diamond Jim stepped off the train and headed to the locomotive engine. He felt much better. Fully alive. Fully in touch with the moment. Seeing every angle of the train's body as he strode forward, hearing the soft grind of his boot soles against the hard plate of the desert as he moved. He felt strong. Bold. Impervious to the heavy heat and dry air that tried to beat him down.

Nothing like a shot of adrenaline to cure a hangover.

He'd been in the mail car when officials of the rail company had secured his money, so he knew the path to get in. It only made sense that the safe was the real target of an assault like this. No one risks a hanging just to hold up a few passengers in their private cars.

It helped that sounds of life had begun to come from up and down the derelict train. Vague voices and occasional crashes came at random moments.

With only one man between himself and personal glory, Jim's thoughts whirled. Money, friends, and publicity. They'd be late getting to

Trinidad, of course, which was annoying, and would piss off Miss Clarisse, who was expecting him to drop a pile of cash in her place tonight. But she'd get over it once she saw the actual pile, and even more so after the papers got out. Clarisse understood how to cash in on relationships. The price of protection was going up, too. "Sheriff" Bernard—Jim's superior—would demand double payments up and down the line for the honor of Jim's oversight.

He'd get it, too.

A badge makes a difference, even as far east as Kansas City.

Overall, things were promising to get quite a bit better for Diamond Jim Walker.

They didn't call him "Diamond," for nothing. But he'd never felt like he had enough money to *really* do whatever he wanted.

If things went well, he could send Cynthia and the kids to the Carolinas for the summer like she'd been pining for. Three months listening to an ocean roar was his personal idea of Hell, but Cynthia swooned every time she talked about it— breathlessly extolling the regenerative powers of salted air and healthy provisions of walks on the beach. Simply watching seagulls and pelicans skim above the ocean waves, she cooed, could settle a mind.

The idea of taking a summer on his own made him happy, too. He approached the locomotive, thinking of headlines. Climbing into the engineer's control room, he found, as expected, the engineer, dead on the floor.

Heart pounding, he slinked through the tender toward the mail car. Quietly opening the door, he found the last bandit, bent down, and peering into the safe. When the door reached full open, the man looked up and straightened.

He was younger than Jim would have imagined, but wiry enough to have been born in the desert itself, wearing a pale blue shirt under a worn vest of heavy weave. So much dust and grime covered his pants that, at first, Jim couldn't peg them as pinstripe. The man's matted hair was the color of sand itself, his eyes a watery blue.

"Do I know you?" Jim said, momentarily confused, but not so much so that he forgot to level the Colt at the man.

"I'm Billy," the man said, raising his hands to show Jim his open palms. "Just checkin' to see things are safe here."

"I see," Jim said.

And he did see. Everything.

He thumbed the Colt to cock the weapon.

"I think I'm about to become a very wealthy man," Jim said.

A shot rang out.

Jim felt like he'd been punched in the gut by something invisible. He couldn't breathe. His chest did something he couldn't explain.

It was like the fist of God had ripped into his ribs to rip out his heart.

He glanced down to see his belly was missing. His fingers went numb. The gun fell to the floor.

He blinked once, and then he was gone.

* * *

Billy watched the hero fall to the floor, knowing he'd see his man Tommy standing behind him. Which he did. They'd been together for a long time. With the Pinkerton gone, Billy knew Tommy'd be around.

Tommy was a big man, but he moved with grace enough that the would-be hero here had missed him.

"Thanks," Billy said.

Tommy put a finger to his hat as he stepped into the mail cart, rifle in hand. "Guess he didn't count us so good."

"Not much for numbers, maybe?" Billy replied.

"Not as much as you seem to be, anyway." Tommy motioned the safe. "Enough to get us to Arizona Country?"

"I don't think so," a woman's voice answered.

The hammers of two guns clicked back.

A woman stood in the hard desert a distance away, revolvers in each hand.

She was not young, but not yet old, either. The skin of her face seemed smooth until Billy looked close enough to see lines at the corners of her lips. She was slim, with long, dark hair that had been sweated through and pasted now at her temples. Her jaw was set. Her gaze was cold as steel.

"Those are some mighty heavy weapons there, Miss," Billy said.

"Hope you can hold 'em," Tommy added.

Her throat pulsed with a swallow.

"This is for Carl," she said.

Two shots rang out.

End Note

You have come to the end of *They Came Back, Stories from the Radius.*

If you enjoyed this book, please consider leaving a review at your favorite online bookseller. Even a few sentences can help!

Acknowledgements

I would like to thank the obvious ones—Ewan "The Guy Who Bought Your First Story" Grantham, and my teachers from DuPont Manual High School, Mr. Abrams and Mr. Sater (Soter?).

I would also like to thank everyone who backed my Kickstarter project that launched this volume that has made me so happy. Without you, it would never have happened.

Michael Barbato-Dunn - Rebecca Buchanan - Michael A. Burstein - Niki Coppola - Laura Rainbow Dragon - Andy F -Jerrie the filkferengi - David H. Hendrickson – Patrick Hay – Lonnie Holder -Kari Kilgore - Joe Lederer - Greg Levick - Michael Warren Lucas - Céline Malgen -Meyari McFarland - Rob McMonigal - Christian Meyer - E.M. Middel - Ronald H. Miller - Alexander Ourique - Brian Pinnell - Mary Jo Rabe - Robert M Ragland - Annie Reed - Carolyn Rowland - Marc Sangalli - Lisa Silverthorne - Dean Wesley Smith - Rob Szarka - Kelly Washington - James Walker (Jwalk) - Keith West, Future Potentate of the Solar System

About Ron Collins

Ron Collins did, indeed, graduate from Manual High School in May 1979. It was, however, a little longer than three weeks before his first book came out. We're not sure he's met the promise his teachers said he had, but he's still working at it, so he has that going for him. In writing, he's heard, practice is of utmost importance.

Along the way, Ron has penned thirty books successfully enough to make him a best-selling author of science fiction and dark fantasy. With his daughter, Brigid, he edited the anthology *Face the Strange*.

His short fiction has received a Writers of the Future prize. His short story "The White Game" was nominated for the Short Mystery Fiction Society's 2016 Derringer Award.

Website

http://www.typosphere.com

Get Free Books!

Join Ron's Reader List

Newsletter: https://typosphere.com/newsletter

Glamour of the God-Touched
(Book 1 of *Saga of the God-Touched Mage*)

STARCRUISE
short story in the *Stealing the Sun* universe

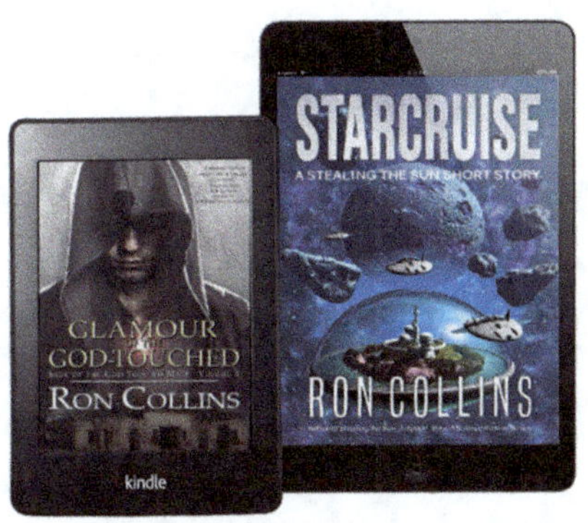